THE LOCALS

Titles in Teen Reads:

Copy Cat
TOMMY DONBAVAND

Dead Scared
TOMMY DONBAVAND

Just Bite
TOMMY DONBAVAND

Home
TOMMY DONBAVAND

Kidnap
TOMMY DONBAVAND

Ward 13
TOMMY DONBAVAND

Deadly Mission
MARK WRIGHT

Ghost Bell
MARK WRIGHT

The Corridor
MARK WRIGHT

Death Road
JON MAYHEW

Fair Game
ALAN DURANT

Jigsaw Lady
TONY LEE

Mister Scratch
TONY LEE

Stalker
TONY LEE

Dawn of the Daves
TIM COLLINS

Joke Shop
TIM COLLINS

The Locals
TIM COLLINS

Troll
TIM COLLINS

Insectoids
ROGER HURN

Billy Button
CAVAN SCOTT

Mama Barkfingers
CAVAN SCOTT

Pest Control
CAVAN SCOTT

The Hunted
CAVAN SCOTT

The Changeling
CAVAN SCOTT

Nightmare
ANN EVANS

Sitting Target
JOHN TOWNSEND

Snow White, Black Heart
JACQUELINE RAYNER

The Wishing Doll
BEVERLY SANFORD

Underworld
SIMON CHESHIRE

World Without Words
JONNY ZUCKER

Badger Publishing Limited, Oldmedow Road, Hardwick Industrial Estate, King's Lynn PE30 4JJ
Telephone: 01438 791037

www.badgerlearning.co.uk

THE LOCALS

TIM COLLINS

The Locals ISBN 978-1-78147-955-1

Publisher: Susan Ross
Senior Editor: Danny Pearson
Publishing Assistant: Claire Morgan
Copyeditor: Cheryl Lanyon
Designer: Bigtop Design Ltd

2 4 6 8 10 9 7 5 3 1

CHAPTER 1

THE MORRIS DANCERS

I was expecting the locals to be weird. But I wasn't expecting them to be this weird.

The men on the village green were wearing white suits and had leaves tied into their hair and beards. They were dancing and tapping sticks in time to accordion music.

A small crowd had gathered to watch them. At least, it seemed small to me. But I'm used to seeing Beyoncé and Alicia Keyes live at the O_2. This was probably a massive crowd by the standards of Hobb's Green.

I'd been sent here to stay with my aunt Carmen while my parents were visiting family back in Jamaica. I was already mad that they didn't trust me to stay home on my own, and sending me to this tiny village had made things worse.

The only shop was the Green Man Post Office; the only place to hang out was the village green; and the only thing to do was watch some beardy weirdies prancing around. Welcome to the lamest place on Earth.

There were only nine other teenagers in the crowd. Five boys, four girls, all dorks. They all had leaves in their hair, just like the Morris dancers.

I tried my best. I really did.

"Hi, I'm Simone," I said.

The locals all kept staring at the Morris dancers.

"I'm from London," I said. "Staying with my aunt Carmen. Do you know her?"

"Lovely lady," said a boy with curly brown hair. He nodded at me, then looked back at the so-called entertainment.

And that was it. No, "How long are you here for?" No, "Tell us about London, that sounds so much cooler than here." Just, "Lovely lady", said in a weird hobbit accent.

I was seething by the time I got back to my aunt's house.

"They wouldn't even talk to me," I said, planting my hands on my hips. "I bet they're closet racists."

My aunt smiled and put her hand on my shoulder. "No they're not. I've been here thirty years and I've never had any problems with that."

You wouldn't think my aunt came from Hackney originally. Not that she'd picked up the local accent, though. She sounded more like the Queen.

I noticed some streaks of green in her hair and looked closer to see she'd tied leaves into her extensions. Nice to see she was joining in with the local 'fashion'.

"They're just a little shy," said my aunt. "But they'll make you feel welcome soon. You'll see."

"I don't like their accents," I said. "They sound stupid."

"Now who's being prejudiced?" she asked.

"I suppose I'll try again," I sighed. "But don't go and talk to them for me. I can fight my own battles."

"I won't," said my aunt. "Promise."

But she did speak to them. I know she did. That's when they started planning the whole awful thing.

CHAPTER 2

THE SPIDER WEB

I'm not sure I should admit this, but I actually tried tucking some leaves under my braids the next day. I looked in the mirror and imagined how my friend Roxy would react.

She would shriek with laughter and shout, "Shame oh shame oh shame oh shame."
That's how.

I pulled them all out. This was one trend I wasn't going to join in with.

It was boiling hot again, so I went out to the Green Man Post Office for a Calippo. Choosing between strawberry and orange had become the most exciting part of my day since I came to the village.

I went for strawberry and wandered slowly back down the road.

I spotted a carving on a wooden beam on the side of a house and stopped to look at it. At first I thought it was just a pile of leaves, but as I stared at it I could make out a face.

It had a scowling mouth, a pointed chin and blank, acorn eyes. Two ferns curled up from its forehead like horns. Was it meant to be the devil? Did someone carve it on their house to keep bad things away?

"Simone!"

I turned to see the boy with curly hair standing on a footpath between two thatched cottages. I was surprised he'd even remembered my name after pretty much blanking me the day before.

"We need you at our youth club," he said, beckoning me over.

I drained the juice from the bottom of the Calippo wrapper, tucked it into a bin and went over to him.

"Quick!" he shouted, turning and running down the narrow path. "I'm Charlie by the way!"

"What's the hurry?" I asked. I followed him, weaving around the nettles that were shooting up from either side.

"The music's about to start," he said.

I liked the sound of this. Maybe Hobb's Green wasn't so pathetic after all.

I checked my pocket for my iPod. Good. If their speaker had Bluetooth I could put the new 'Now' compilation on. There was bound to be something on there they'd like.

The footpath turned out to be a shortcut to the village green.

All the local teens were gathered around a huge wooden pole, grasping blue, green and yellow ribbons that were tied to the top.

"You found her," shouted a girl with oak leaves tied into her long, red hair. She ran over to a cassette player, clicked it on and muddy accordion music blasted out.

A cassette player?

I've heard of hipsters collecting vinyl, but I didn't think cassettes even existed any more. It's just as well I didn't bother asking those bumpkins about Bluetooth.

Charlie held out a thick, green strip of ribbon.

"Take your position," he shouted.

I looked around. The other girls were standing close to the pole and facing out, while the boys were standing further away and facing in. I took the ribbon and jumped into a gap by the pole.

"We're doing the Spider Web," said the girl with red hair.

"I have totally no idea what that is," I said.

"Stand still," said Charlie, "and watch what we do, 'cause you'll be doing it next."

The boys wove in and out of us in time with the music until the ribbons made a huge, multi-coloured spider web.

I imagined the grief I'd get if a photo of this got out. Even the nerdiest gang in school would cast me out.

"Turn!" shouted Charlie.

The boys went back the other way, untangling the web.

I doubted there'd be much chance of this ending up on Instagram, though. If they were still using cassettes, smart phones were probably ten years away.

"Now you!" shouted Charlie.

It was our turn to weave around the boys. I went the wrong way a couple of times, but I soon got the hang of it.

And that was it. That was all we did at youth club. Dancing back and forth. Making a web, unmaking a web.

But you know what? I actually sort of got into it. I've always liked dancing, but I think it was more than that. Something about taking part in an old tradition made me feel proud.

I feel stupid about that now, of course.

We kept dancing as the sun climbed higher. I felt hot and a little dizzy. I started to feel like I was being watched. I couldn't shake the feeling that angry eyes were staring at me, even though there was no one else around but the maypole dancers.

Then I spotted it. The same leafy devil face I'd seen on the house had been carved near the top of the pole. Its cold, acorn eyes seemed to follow me as I skipped around it.

CHAPTER 3

THE VISITOR

I went for a walk after I'd eaten my Calippo the next day.

If I go for a walk in London, it's usually around Westfield Shopping Centre or to Roxy's flat. I never walk just for the sake of it, with nowhere to go and no one to see. But it was another hot day and I was already starting to feel more at home in Hobb's Green.

A path opposite the Post Office sloped down to a stream. I walked alongside the water for a few minutes before plonking myself on a patch of soft grass.

My sit soon turned to a lie and my eyelids began to feel heavy. I unzipped my top, shoved it under my head and closed my eyes.

I could hear the flowing of the stream, the cawing of birds high above and distant accordion music from the village. They were Morris dancing again, or skipping around the maypole.

I wondered if I'd been wrong to think that all that stuff was lame. I'd always wanted the newest music, the newest trainers and the newest phone, but I was starting to see the appeal of really old things too.

I must have drifted off while I was thinking about this because the next thing I can remember is a pile of leaves and twigs blowing over and forming themselves into the same devilish face I'd seen in the carvings.

The face fixed its cold, acorn eyes on me, opened its leaf mouth and let out a high giggle. The leaves on its cheeks and forehead flapped open and I could see spiders, ants and flies writhing underneath. The acorn eyes cracked open like eggs to reveal writhing, pink earthworms.

"Queen of the May," said the face in a high, delirious voice.

I woke up with my heart hammering in my chest. I tried to open my eyes, but found I couldn't do it. In fact, I couldn't move at all. My arms, legs and mouth were all paralysed.

This happens to me in the night sometimes and I hate it. It felt even worse outside and in an unfamiliar place.

Sometimes I can snap out of it by focusing all my attention on my right arm. I move that, and I suddenly find I can move everything else again.

I tried, but it didn't budge. I was weak and frozen under the beating sun.

The accordion seemed to be getting louder and I thought I could hear someone skipping towards me.

I tried to focus my energy on my right eyelid instead. If I could force it open, maybe that would get me moving.

The music really was getting louder. I wasn't imagining it. Someone was hopping towards me and playing the accordion.

I finally managed to force my eye open and a dark-green shape came into focus.

A tall, lumbering figure was hopping from foot to foot. He was completely covered in fresh, green leaves, from his stout legs to the thick fingers that were jabbing at his accordion. His face was a rippling mass of green with no eyes or mouth.

At last the strength came back into my body. I opened my mouth and screamed.

CHAPTER 4

THE MAY QUEEN

"Sorry," said the figure. "I wasn't trying to frighten you."

I recognised the voice as Charlie's. He dropped his accordion and took his mask off. His face was red and his curly hair was flattened down. He grinned at me.

I got up and rubbed the pins and needles out of my arms.

"I didn't mean to scream," I said. "You just woke me up, that's all."

"Oops-a-daisy," he said.

I pointed to his costume with its layers of leaves pinned to loose cloth. It seemed a weird one to make. How long would it last without going rotten?

"What's this for?" I asked.

"The parade tomorrow," he said. A wide smile spread over his face. "It's my turn to be the Green Man."

"That must be nice for you," I said. "Whatever that means."

I grabbed my top and shook the grass off it.

"It's a tradition," said Charlie. "We do it every year. And I've got some good news for you. We've chosen you to be the May Queen."

"Thanks," I said. "I think. What do I have to do?"

"Nothing," he said. "Just sit on a chair while the men from the village carry you from the Post Office to the green. Don't you have parades in London?"

"We have the Notting Hill Carnival," I said. "But I don't think it's the same sort of thing."

You should have seen my aunt's face when I got back and told her I was going to be May Queen. You'd think I'd got straight A-stars in my exams and a place in 'The X Factor' final.

"That's amazing," she said, grabbing my hands. "You must be so pleased."

"I suppose so," I said.

"May Queen!" she said, pressing my nose. "There are girls in this village who've been waiting all their lives for that. They'll be so jealous. What clothes have you got with you?"

I thought about my suitcase. "My DKNY jeans, my Guess jeans, my Diesel top, my Hollister top, my Adidas cap…"

"It doesn't matter," she said. "I'll find the dress I wore when I was May Queen. I know I kept it. Just go and pick some wild flowers to freshen it up. You'll need buttercups, bluebells, forget-me-nots..."

And that's how I found myself in the forest behind my aunt's garden gathering flowers I didn't know the names of for a parade I didn't understand the point of. But being May Queen was better than being ignored by everyone, I supposed.

May Queen.

Queen of the May.

Had I heard those words in my dream before Charlie had spoken them?

I plucked a blue flower and sniffed it. I reckoned it was probably a bluebell.

Something flitted between the thick trunks ahead of me. It looked like Charlie, dressed in his leaf costume again. But he was moving much more gracefully now.

"Charlie!" I shouted. "What are you doing?"

I heard light footsteps behind and span round to see him leaping between two oak trees.

"Charlie!" I shouted again. I dropped my flowers and ran over to the trees. But there was no one there. I was alone in the forest.

CHAPTER 5

THE DRESS

My aunt strode into my room at seven the next morning and flung the curtains open.

I winced and pulled the covers over my head. I hate waking up early. I don't even do it on school days. I get up at 8.15, shove my clothes on and run for the 8.25 bus.

"How's the May Queen feeling?" asked my aunt. I peeped out from the covers and saw she was wearing a long, white robe. "Excited about the parade?"

"Fine," I said, rubbing my eyes. "Do you always sleep in that gown?"

"This isn't a gown," she said. "It's my procession costume. Talking of which…"

She went into her room and came back in with an old-fashioned, long, white dress with frilly sleeves. "This is for you."

I imagined the howls of laughter from Roxy if she ever saw me wearing it.

"They won't take any photos will they?" I asked. "I don't want my friends back in London to see this."

"I'm sure your friends would respect our traditions," said my aunt. "They don't tease girls who wear headscarves, do they?"

"No," I said. "But that's religious."

"This is too," said my aunt, wandering back to her room. "In a way. But no, they won't take photos. We like to keep ourselves to ourselves here."

I swung my legs out of bed, sat up and examined the dress. It was pretty tatty. Some of the lace on the front had gone yellow, and there were brown spots and green streaks on the sleeves.

"Are you sure you've washed this?" I shouted.

"Sorry about the grass stains," she said. "They're left over from when I became May Queen. That's still one of the best days of my life, you know."

I glanced at the row of porcelain figurines on my aunt's windowsill. From a distance I'd thought they were all white women in big, old-fashioned dresses. The sort of tacky stuff my grandma loves. But on closer inspection I could see their faces were made from tiny sculpted leaves, and they all had lifeless, acorn eyes, just like the carvings in the village.

"What do you reckon?"

I turned to look at my aunt and gasped. Her face had been replaced by a mess of leaves.

"It's my mask," she said. "For the parade."

She lifted it off. It was a cloth hood with fresh leaves stuck to it, like the one Charlie had been wearing.

"Tell me I don't have to wear one of those," I said.

"Of course not," she said. "We need to see the May Queen's face. That's part of it."

I looked down at the brown spots on the sleeves. Now that I looked at them again, they seemed deep red. The colour blood goes when it dries.

CHAPTER 6

THE PARADE

"What's that for?" I asked.

One of the men was binding my arms to the side of a chair with a bright green ribbon. The chair was stuck to long poles, making it look like the sort of thing an ancient emperor would have been carried in.

"So you don't fall off," he said, pulling the ribbon tight and tying a knot in it. "Health and Safety."

I heard several of the others chuckling behind their leaf masks.

"I'm not sure I want to go ahead with this," I said.

"I was nervous too," said my aunt. She was wearing her white robe and green mask, and I could only tell her apart from the others by her hands. "But you'll soon forget yourself and enjoy it."

"I don't think I will," I said.

The locals had been waiting for us outside the Post Office. They were all wearing robes and masks, except Charlie, who was wearing his full-body suit and carrying his accordion.

No one was wearing shoes. My aunt had told me to go barefoot too, but I'd ignored her. After I'd decorated my dress with wild flowers, I looked at myself in the mirror and decided to wear all my normal clothes underneath so I could take the stupid thing off as soon as the parade was over.

The men hoisted my chair into the air. I was flung from side to side as they walked down the uneven road.

A group of the locals broke to the front of the procession and waved hankies around as they skipped along. Children in smaller robes and masks trailed behind, skipping and giggling.

I could see my aunt at the side, clapping her hands above her head as if she was in church. I thought it would make me feel less awkward to know she was part of this, but it didn't. She was just as weird as the rest of them.

The locals jumped, twirled and threw their hands in the air as we made our way to the green.

I couldn't begin to imagine how Roxy would react if she saw this. I thought she'd probably laugh herself to death.

Charlie leaped to the very front of the parade. He was twirling high in the air like a ballet dancer without missing a single note on his accordion. I'd have been impressed if I wasn't so freaked out by it all.

I started to notice those leaf faces everywhere as we went on. There were stone faces peering down from drains like angry gargoyles, there were vague carvings in weather-beaten wood and I even spotted a couple of garden gnomes with leaf skin and acorn eyes.

We arrived at the green and Charlie leaped around, prancing nimbly and playing his accordion.

I thought the men would put me down now, but they carried me right into the middle and held me up high.

"Alright," I said. I could feel my pulse speeding up. "Parade's over."

The locals formed a circle around me, held hands and hummed along to the jaunty accordion tune.

I scanned the circle for my aunt. I had to twist my head round to find her. "What's going on now? It's finished, hasn't it?"

"Of course not!" shouted my aunt. "It's time for you to become May Queen."

"Queen of the May!" shouted a high, mischievous voice in front of me.

The crowd hummed louder and began to swing their linked arms up and down.

"I'm getting sick of this," I shouted. A bead of sweat trickled down my forehead into my eye, but I couldn't wipe it away. "Untie me now!"

The locals hummed louder.

"Auntie Carmen!" I shouted. "Tell them to untie me!"

I tried to pull my arms out of the ribbons, but they held tight.

"Take me down, you stupid bumpkins!" I shouted in an uneven voice. "I don't want to stay in this pathetic little backwater. I want to go back to civilisation. I don't want to be your May Queen."

Charlie broke away from the crowd and pranced towards me.

"Charlie!" I shouted. "Stop this now. Joke's over."

He lowered the accordion to the floor. The humming cut out and the locals fell still.

"Finally," I said. "Someone's listened to me."

I could hear Charlie giggling behind his mask. It was a high, shrieking sound. Not the sort of laugh I'd have expected him to have.

"Take that mask off and talk to me," I said.

Charlie lifted his hands up to his cloth hood and peeled it off.

There wasn't a curly-haired white boy underneath, but more green. At first I thought he had another mask on, but then I realised it was a long, grinning face made from leaves.

This wasn't Charlie at all. This was *him*. The one I'd seen all those carvings of.

CHAPTER 7

THE GREEN MAN

I stared at the figure in front of me. Thin branches sprouting red berries were growing out of his nostrils, ears and tear ducts. His slanting brows were made from fine roots and there were patches of moss around his acorn eyes. Tiny flies and ticks crawled around the oak leaves that swept across his forehead, cheeks and chin.

Everyone in the circle bowed and chanted, "Hail to the Green Man."

"Take me down," I screamed.

The locals carried me nearer to him. I could hear my pulse beating in my ears as I tried to yank my wrists free.

"Queen of the May," shrieked the Green Man. He shed his bulky cotton costume to reveal a lean body of twisting branches, thick vines and emerald leaves. "Queen of the May! Queen of the May!"

He hopped towards me in a lightning-fast Morris dance and held out his right arm.

"Queen of the May!"

A sharp branch ripped out of his wrist and shot towards me. I tried to pull back, but the ribbons held firm. The Green Man squealed out a laugh as the branch coiled around my arm and the arm of the chair.

"Stop it, you leafy freak!" I shouted. The branch squeezed my arm like a snake. "Let me go!"

“Don’t resist!” shouted my aunt from behind me. “Let him take over. You won’t regret it.”

Sharp thorns sprouted from the branch and broke my skin with bright flashes of pain.

“Why are you doing this?” I screamed. I tried to wriggle free but the thorns cut deeper.

I heard Charlie’s voice from near my feet. All the time I’d thought he’d been in the bulky costume, he’d been one of the robed men carrying my chair. “If you let the Green Man into your heart you’ll see why we love him. You’ll love him too, and you’ll want to bring him new followers just like we do.”

As the thorns dug into my skin, an image of the Green Man hopping through thick woodland came into my mind. Then an image of him leading a procession of ancient people in animal skins.

I tried to force these pictures out.

The Green Man fixed his acorn eyes on me and giggled.

"You're a parasite," I shouted. "You feed off the worship of gullible idiots like this lot. But I'm not going to fall for it. I think you're just as much of a tragic yokel as the rest of them."

"Don't fight it!" shouted my aunt. "You'll feel such joy."

Images of people from long-gone ages dancing, parading and skipping swept into my mind. I felt a sudden swell of love for these old traditions.

How long did anything last these days before it went out of fashion or needed an upgrade? Wouldn't it be better to be part of something that went back thousands of years? Why didn't I just give in and let myself worship him?

I fought these feelings. The Green Man was planting these thoughts in my mind. They weren't mine.

I concentrated on London, desperately trying to replace the ancient images.

I thought about going down to Westfield for the sales and loading up with plastic bags. I thought about going to Shoreditch with Roxy to mingle with hipsters. I thought about queuing outside the O_2 to get right to the front for Jay Z. That was my world. Not this place.

"Queen of the May," hissed the Green Man. His smile dropped and his mossy brow knotted above his acorn eyes. "Queen of the May."

The branch around my wrist gripped tighter and the thorns cut deeper. A vision of Victorian men and women dancing around a maypole came into my mind. I felt joy welling inside me again, but I fought it. It was a filthy, false joy and I didn't want it.

I took a deep breath and lunged sideways. The men holding my chair buckled, but held their grip.

"Stop struggling!" shouted Charlie. "Give in to him."

I tried again. This time they tumbled to the floor.

The branch connecting me to the green man snapped, and I hit the ground with a crack that jolted my entire body. Both arms of the chair splintered into wooden shards and I yanked them away. I pulled my arms free of the ribbons and the coiled branch and got to my feet.

The Green Man was staring down at the broken branch coming from his hand and yowling. Green sap was squirting from it like blood from a burst artery.

"Queen of the May!" he shrieked.

"Queen of the May!" chanted the locals, closing in on me.

I charged at them.

CHAPTER 8

THE ROAD

I tugged my dress over my head as I ran down the track. Wild flowers shook loose as I dragged it away.

After I'd forced my way out of the circle of locals, I'd headed for the stoniest, bumpiest track I could find. I was the only one wearing trainers, and I wanted to make the most of the advantage.

I threw the dress to the floor and looked over my shoulder. Sure enough, the locals were falling behind. But there was one figure racing ahead. The Green Man was sprinting with his acorn eyes fixed on me. Leaves and berries were blowing away from his branches as he dashed.

The track ran along a field with a dozen cows in it. A couple of them were looking up, but the rest kept grazing. A long hedge marked the far edge of the field and I could see cars flitting through the gaps.

It was a road. Not a very big one. But it would lead to a bigger one, which would lead to a motorway, which would lead back to London.

I pelted up to the hedge and searched for the thinnest spot. I launched myself through, scraping my arms and neck. One of my braids got stuck on a twig and I stopped to untangle it with shaking fingers, knowing that the Green Man was silently gaining on me.

I dragged myself out of the hedge and jogged down the side of the road. A car was coming.

I glanced back and saw blank, acorn eyes peeping through the gap in the hedge. The Green Man had caught up.

I ran into the middle of the road and waved my arms. The car skidded to a halt just a couple of feet away and a woman with glasses stared at me with her mouth open.

The Green Man tried to leap through the hedge, but one of the vines on his leg caught on a branch. He reached down and snapped it, wincing with pain.

I ran round to the passenger door. The woman leaned over to lock it, but I managed to get inside.

"I don't have any money," she said.

"I don't want any," I said, slamming the door closed. "I just want you to drive me away from here."

Tears were welling in my eyes and I couldn't see very clearly, but I could tell the shape of the Green Man was approaching fast.

"Please!" I shouted. "Now!"

The woman turned the key and the car pulled away just as twig fingers scraped the back window. As I blinked the tears away, I caught a glimpse of the Green Man's furious, acorn eyes for the last time.

"Was that a tree?" asked the woman.

"Must have been," I said.

*

I'm back home now and looking out of my window at the London skyline. My parents still think I'm in Hobb's Green and I'm going to let them keep thinking it.

I doubt my aunt will be in any hurry to tell them I've come back either. As she says, they like to keep themselves to themselves up there. The last thing they want is some outsider spreading rumours about how they worship an ancient pile of leaves.

You know what? Let them keep doing their freaky thing. I'm just never, ever going back.

Tomorrow I'm meeting Roxy in Westfield. We're going to hang out in the Food Court, where I won't be able to see a single leaf or blade of grass in any direction. Sounds perfect.

THE END